SEASONED WITH *Grace*

ESSIE SQUARE

Seasoned With Grace
Copyright © 2020 by Essie Square. All rights reserved.

No part of this publication may be reproduced, stored in a retrieval system or transmitted in any way by any means, electronic, mechanical, photocopy, recording or otherwise without the prior permission of the author except as provided by USA copyright law.

This novel is a work of fiction. Names, descriptions, entities, and incidents included in the story are products of the author's imagination. Any resemblance to actual persons, events, and entities is entirely coincidental.

The opinions expressed by the author are not necessarily those of URLink Print and Media.

1603 Capitol Ave., Suite 310 Cheyenne, Wyoming USA 82001
1-888-980-6523 | admin@urlinkpublishing.com

URLink Print and Media is committed to excellence in the publishing industry.

Book design copyright © 2020 by URLink Print and Media. All rights reserved.

Published in the United States of America

ISBN 978-1-64753-313-7 (Paperback)
ISBN 978-1-64753-314-4 (Digital)

21.03.20

In a personal physical position of humility.
I find myself tried by time, and other
factors of pure emotional and spiritual stresses.
I write to say: I am blessed.

Essie Square

CHAPTER 1

It's Monday morning, and Paul had just spent a wonderful and peaceful weekend with his family. After working a heavy schedule, the past week. As attending emergency room physician at John Hopkin's Hospital. Paul needed the rest, and enjoyed the time off with his family. Smiling, Paul turns over in bed to the feel of Mary, running her hands down to the side of his face. Feeling good, he groans, leaning in for their morning kiss. Still smiling, Paul gets out of bed and heads toward the bathroom to prepare for work. Picking up one of Mary's slippers on the floor, he throws it at her still form buried beneath the bed covers. "Get up sleepy head". Mary ignoring Paul, buried herself deeper under the bedcovers. A few minutes later groaning, Mary gets up, heading towards their sons' room, to get them ready for breakfast and school. Paul's job this morning was to make breakfast. He and Mary took turns making breakfast, while the other got the boys ready for school. And hour later, Paul is driving Mary and their two sons to the day care center, where Mary works as administrator. Driving into the day care entrance, Paul leans over and kiss Mary, then unbuckling, gets out taking the boys out of their car seats. Smiling Paul bends down, kissing both boys on top of their heads. "I love you guys, stay out of trouble and look out for your mother for me, you hear?" the twin boys nod their heads smiling. After watching them go into the day care center. Paul continues to his job at the hospital. Enjoying a mood of contentment as he drives his Land Rover into his parking space in the hospital emergency room staff area. Thinking about what a beautiful family and life he has made for himself. Comparing them to the other staff members that he works with here at John Hopkins. The horror stories of drug abuse, divorces, runaway kids and broken homes. Paul is reminded of the beautiful wife he has. Their boys and lovely home. Remembering how he first met Mary, Paul glances down at his watch, and sees that he has thirty-two minutes before his shift began. He slides down in his seat, closes his eyes, and lets his mind, take him back to his college days with his twin brother Peter. Paul, running down the hallway of his college dormitory, calls out to Peter to hurry up. Their dad was coming to pick them up in twenty minutes. He didn't like waiting on the boys every time he came to pick them up from school on holidays, and school breaks, He would always find them not ready on his arrival. Paul had all of his bags sitting on the sidewalk waiting for their dad on this time. Turning towards the dorm to call Peter, Paul observed Mary, one of his dorm mates, sitting alone on the side stairways looking depressed. Paul began walking towards Mary. "Hi Mary, are you waiting for your parents' to pick you up too?" Mary looks up at Paul with those big brown eyes, that he later always got lost in. Responded with a shrug of her shoulders. "Paul, you seem to forget that I have no parents." Paul sighing, "Oh Mary, I am so sorry, I forgot. I was not trying to be insensitive. Mary, I understand. My brother Peter is a friend of yours here, and you are in his circle of friends. Peter has told me in privacy." Mary looking away, tells Paul that she will be staying at the orphanage for the holiday break. The staff appears to enjoy her help, seeing that she doesn't have any relatives. Peter sat beside Mary, continued in conversation, waiting on his brother and father to arrive.

Angela was busy putting the finishing touch on the Thanksgiving turkey in the oven. When she heard the noise of her boys and husband John entering the front door. Wiping her hands on her apron, Angela turns around as John approaches her with a hug and kiss. With the boys following close behind him. "Well it's about time you guys arrived. I thought I would have to put an all-points bulletin out on you three." While Angela was still speaking, she notices a small framed young woman, standing beside the front door in a state of fright and distress. Angela stopped talking, looking at her husband for answers as to who the young woman was. Paul ran to his mother. Hugging and kissing her cheeks, pulling Mary towards his mother for introductions.

CHAPTER 2

With the honking horn of a staff member parking beside Paul, he was pulled out of his day dreaming of how Mary became a constant part of his family 4 years ago, and after their graduations, she became his wife.

Still smiling, Paul waves to the other emergency room staff member, as he locks his Land Rover door. It is now 6:00 AM, and Paul's workday has begun, as he enters John Hopkins Hospital emergency room, as one of the attending physicians. Back at the day care center, Mary settles down with a class. One of her teachers did not report to work, and could not be reached by telephone. Mary has to take over her class of 3-year-olds. Mary's sons were in that class. Their day appeared to be moving along nicely.

Back at John Hopkins Emergency room, Paul's shift took off rapidly. It is 10 AM, and Paul have not been able to take a break yet. The emergency room has been filled all morning long with all types of injuries and sicknesses, needing his immediate attention. At approximately 10 AM, the emergency room dispatcher received a call that a gunshot victim was in route with multiple gunshot wounds. Eight minutes later, the emergency room door opens for the victim and paramedics, accompanied by policemen. Paul and the waiting emergency room staff quickly grabs the victim, running through the emergency entrance area, to the acute trauma and surgical room to save his life. Paul and emergency room staff, long with the surgical staff, works for hours until they stabilized the man. He is then sent to the intensive care unit for further monitoring and care. A policeman was placed outside at the intensive care unit tor security. An officer was placed inside of the room for staff protections as well. Paul was leaving the intensive care unit returning to the emergency room. Wondering what had happened to cause all the trauma to the young Man. When he was met at the elevators by the hospital administrator, requesting him to join him in his office.

Paul exhausted, and in need of a cup of coffee and a break, followed the director back to his orifice. On passing the emergency room, Paul could sense something was wrong by the body language of the emergency room staff with no one making eye contact with him as they pass by. Wondering what was going on, Paul could see a group of police officers, and his brother standing in the hallway leading to the

director's office. Paul looking at his brother Peter. "Why are you here? What's going on?" The director goes over to the police officer, and speaks quietly to them, then turns to escort Paul and his brother Peter into his office, closing the door behind them. A few minutes later, a loud scream could he heard coming from behind the closed door. Then a thud as someone is heard falling. The scene inside the director's office was one of chaos and pain, that Paul's brother wished he never had to experience, just as the one he had to play out when their father died, but here he was again in the hot seat. Peter had not liked to be in the role of big brother to Paul, because they were born only a few minutes apart they were told. Peter was here consoling his brother, after delivering him such devastating news, of how, in one day, the single act of an angry man, had taken the life of his entire family. The director had to finish telling Paul what had happened, Peter could not get his tongue to continue forming such horrible words.

The director asked Paul to sit down, but Paul would not sit. Finally, he sat as are director begun to talk, explaining to Paul what had happened. After dropping Mary and the boys off at the day care center. It appears that one of the day care teachers was being terrorized by her husband. Fearing for her and her daughter's lives, she didn't show up for work this morning. Mary took her class of three-year-old's. The husband intoxicated and high on methamphetamine came into the center with a gun looking for them. When Mary told him that she didn't show up for work that morning, and for him to leave, or she would call the police, the man drew his gun, killing Mary and three of the children. Paul's two sons was killed with Mary and another child. The other teachers locked, and barricaded their rooms until the police arrived. Paul could feel a sense of all feeling slowly leaving his body, and he could hear what sounded like someone screaming at a distance, till he couldn't hear them anymore.

Paul could feel a hand on his face. Thinking that it was Mary. Thinking that it was Mary, running her hands down his cheeks, the way she would wake him every morning. Paul smiled, turning his face into the hands, only to open his eyes looking into the grey eyes of his mother Angela. Paul starts to cry, as grief came, crowding out everything else. Seeing all the pain and suffering mirrored there in his mother's eyes. Paul turned his body and face towards the wall. Feeling as if his been had been ripped from his chest. Leaving only a gapping empty whole, and him, a shell of a man overwhelmed in sensations, knowing that he had just saved the life of the man that took the life of his family.

Angela had received the tragic and devastating news. Of the deaths or Mary and her grandsons from Peter. The brothers were twins, and had always been inseparable all the way through college, and their marriages. But as time passed, they seemed to grow apart. Then with the death at their father, and his marriage to Mary, they just stopped talking to each other. No matter how hard she tried to get answers from them, they were quiet on the matter and drifted apart. Their three times a year family visits on her birthday in February, Christmas, and Thanksgiving just stopped when Paul married Mary and had the boys, their visits stopped altogether. Angela asked 'Why?" The answer was always the same. From Paul it was, "Busy working at the hospital, trying to get ahead." Peter always answered her with, "My business has me travelling all the time, mother." from Peter. So, Angela finally stopped asking.

Angela, since the death at their father John three years ago. Angela dedicated her lite to doing missionary work to keep busy, and keep the loneliness of missing John away. Their father John was not born in America. He was born in London England. She had met John while taking a vacation to France with some of her friends, from her first job after college. Working as an administrative assistant to the American embassy in France. John was there visiting with his father from London. John's rather was a government official, doing business at the Embassy. John was left to himself, to ramble around France on his own. That's how he and Angela accidentally collided into each other, while she was on her lunch break. Alter wiping the food off his clothing that Angela was carrying when they collided into each other, the two introduced themselves. Becoming inseparable for the next two weeks of John and his father visit. The two was married a year later, with John moving to the United States, and leaving his father back in London. John and Angela wanted to do humanitarian work. For John's parents were devoted to Missionary work. He and Angela began to do missionary work in poor undeveloped countries, and for the next several years, sponsored by their home town church. The two enjoyed the work they were able to provide. After their return to the United States, they settled down and began their family. John was appointed chairman of the national missionary board. For the next twenty-three years their lives seemed complete. Their sons Peter and Paul grew into strong mature men, married and began to raise their own families.

Two years ago, John lost his life in a tragic fall from their church balcony stairway. While doing some light carpentry work. Suffering a massive heart attack afterward. After John's death, Angela returned

John's remains back to his family in England, to be buried with his parents, for John was their only child, and they had died some years before, leaving only distance relatives which she did not know.

Their sons had shared a close father-son relationship. The sudden death of their father John, was like a freight turn had come barreling right through their lives. Destroying, separating, and crushing everything in front of it.

Coming out oi her thoughts, Angela knew she had a long and hard situation ahead oi her. With the funeral arrangements to be made, and Mary an orphan with no known relatives, with Peter's help, they will get his brother Paul through this coining week.

CHAPTER 3

Five days have passed since that tragic day which caused Paul to lose everything that he thought was life to him. Angela watching her son grieving for his family, was at times more that she could take. Seeing him wandering around the house examining personal belongings of Mary. The smell of their bed sheets, and pillow where Mary had laid. Not allowing his mother to change or wash any of Mary's things. Paul would take her unwashed clothing's from the laundry hamper, gathering them around him in their bed trying to keep her close to him at night. He would find himself wandering down the hallway to the boy's room, listening at their closed door for their small voices as they laugh and played with each other after they had been put to bed at night. Thinking that Paul and their mother Mary was asleep.

The house, now empty, void of Mary smiling at him, and no sons to grab his legs, calling "Daddy" as he entered the house after work. Sitting in his bedroom void of feelings. He wonders what will he do with himself.

On the day of the memorial service, Paul could not find courage to get dressed, or even get out of bed at his mother's persistent urging. Peter and Angela had been the buffer for him dealing with making all the arrangements, including relatives, friends, hospital staff, and the news media. With this being such a tragic and high-profile case in the city. Everyone respected the family wishes. Keeping their distance. Out of respect for Paul. His loss and grief. The memorial service is to be held in the church chapel at 10:00 AM, and Paul is still in his room not dressed, Angela is at her wits end with Paul, so she calls Peter for help. Peter arrives at the house, enters Paul's bedroom, closing the door on a distraught Angela. Goes into the bathroom, turns the shower on, walks back to Paul's bed, pulls the covers off, yelling at Paul to get up. Paul looking up at his brother from the bed, grabs the covers again, yelling back at him to leave his house. Peter feeling defeated and hurt, sits on the side of Paul's bed, dropping his head, and in a quiet voice reminds his brother that he wasn't the only one that lost a family on that faithful and tragic day. Reminding Paul that he and their mother Angela lost a family too. But is here with him as the remaining family, and today they had to put their strength together to lay their family to rest. Peter reminded Paul of all the oaths they had made growing up. To be there for each other, no matter what came about in each other lives. That was a blood vow they had made, one day as young boys in their tree house. And now as men in their real houses, they are bound to carry it through.

An hour later...

Paul and Peter come out of the bedroom, dressed for the memorial service. Their mother looks up from the couch where she waiting. Even though her face is strained from the pain and grief, she smiles at her sons standing together like they use to do while growing up. The memorial service had taken its toll on the family, especially Paul. Relatives and friends were there to help out throughout the service and the fellowship afterwards. After everyone had cleaned up and made their condolences and left Paul's home, Angela wanted to know if Paul needed anything before, she retired to her room to rest. The activities of the day had taken a toll on her, leaving her with body aches, no appetite and tiredness. Dealing with everything that had been happening since her arrival, Angela had taken to frequent naps early in the evening, something sherd never done before. She thought it was maybe brought on by all the stress. She vowed to get a check tip on her return back home.

Angela wakes up that Sunday morning, feeling more refreshed than she had felt in a long time. A month has passed after the memorial services for Paul's family. Angela thought that it was time for Paul to begin to process his grief. She knew that the trial of the man who took the life of her family members would start in a couple of months, and Paul would need to have gathered some strength to deal with the trial, To start figuring out how he is going to carry on with the rest of his life_ Angela has spent a month away from her home. and the fife she continued to have within the church, after her husband's death. Keeping herself busy within the church missions, had taken a lot of the loneliness away. Dedicating her time to helping others, gave Angela a feeling of self-worth again... Knowing that someone still needed and wanted her help.

Preparing breakfast, Angela thinks of how she and her husband had raised their sons. John had been a devout head deacon and humanitarian. Using the massive wealth left him by his parents to help others. Raising his sons in the same order. Angela wondered what went wrong. After their father died, the boys began to stray away from the home life, she and their father had made for them. Instead, spending most of their free time away from home with their friends. They would not go back to church after their father lost his life there. They refused to talk to her about it.

Looking up from the breakfast table and seeing Paul, Angela smiles, recognizing the strained look on his face. Of not getting enough sleep. Despite spending all day shut up in his room. Paul sitting down to eat with her at the dinner table, for the first time since Mary and the children death, is a good thing Angela thinks. That this is a good time to discuss Paul's future plans with him. "Paul would you like to attend church service with me this morning?" It has been three weeks since the death of his family, and Angela is curious about the mental and emotional challenges facing her son. Paul began to eat his breakfast, looking up at Angela as he ate. Angela asked Paul when was he planning on returning to work. If he needed her to do anything in the house before she left the following week for home.

Paul quietly looks around the room. as if he is confused. Then looking at his mother, he tells her no, he does not want to go to church, and he has no idea when he will be going back to work. Dropping his fork into his plate, Paul begins to sob into his hands and covers his face_ Angela knew at that moment she could not leave her son in the condition he's in. She has to get him help the best and only way she knew how.

CHAPTER 4

A knock cameo on the door of his office, as pastor Davis sat in his study, looking over a sermon he was preparing for the young men convention coming up in two weeks. Pastor Davis walks to his door, wondering who is visiting him without calling, and making an appointment with the secretary. For everyone knows how busy he is at the moment.

Opening the door, he is surprised to be looking into the face of an old friend, he hasn't seen in thirty years. Angela and her husband John had been the best of friends to he and his wife Daisy. Both couples serving together as missionaries in Africa over thirty-four years ago. Pastor Davis is glad to see an old friend alter so many years has passed. but is anxious concerning the visit.

He greets Angela, and invites her into his study, wondering what has caused her to appear so suddenly, and without calling, and without her husband John. Angela could read Pastor Davis thoughts as he offered her a seat. Pastor Davis asked Angela what brought her to his door after so many years? Angela begins to bring him up to data as he leans in, capturing her every word.

The rest of the week goes along smoothly. Angela calls her church and explains the problem that her family is experiencing, and they assured her that the church would be in constant intercessory prayer for her family. That everything would work out for their good as true believers. It is Saturday morning; Angela received a call from Pastor Davis. requesting a home visit that Saturday evening if Paul was not working... Angela assured Pastor Davis she would make sure that he was home when he arrived.

Paul had a habit of going out around six PM every night that he was not working, and corning back late. Sneaking by her, going to his room, and to bed. Angela knew those habits, for she had done the very same thing for the two years after John's death. Until one-night driving in a drunken state, she nearly took the life of a small child. She vowed to God to never touch another drink for the rest of her life. Repenting and dedicating the rest of her life to helping and not harming others. Angela never told her children about her drinking after their father's death. She didn't want them to know that she was so weak. Angela had kept so many secrets from them. And this was just another one added to her lists of secrets. Angela believed that was why her husband John spent so much money and time within the church. Trying to make restitutions for his and their sins. Yes, two years later Angela knew the signs.

The doorbell rings, and Angela goes to answer it, calling out to Paul that they had company. Pastor Davis enters the home of Paul, shakes hands with Angela and Paul. Angela introduces them, offering Pastor Davis a seat. Paul looks at Pastor Davis wondering how this conversation will end.

Angela excuses herself, going into the kitchen to make a pot of fresh coffee for their guest, leaving the two men to talk and get acquainted with each other. Angela made sure that she stayed long enough for Pastor Davis to get the attention of Paul. She believed the private conversation that exchanged between them in his office this past week, and what Pastor Davis would witness to Paul, will change Paul's life in a positive way this evening. Helping him to get on with his life. Angela is thanking God for little favors. Pastor Davis knows that this young man's future is being put into his hands again by God. And every word that comes out of his mouth has to be seasoned with grace and God's love. being led by the Holy Spirit. Pastor Davis sitting across from Paul began to unveil a part of his life that he had locked up in secret keepings with much prayer. Having put away those secrets many years ago in the hope to save this young man that meant so much to him. With eyes of pain and regret Pastor Davis starts to talk. " Paul, just like you. I lost the love of my life in one day. My wife and I served as missionaries over 30 years ago. We were young, and wanted to go overseas to a non-Christian country to help bring others to the Lord, and help the less fortunate. After completing our mission with the Church, we came back to the United States, and I was installed as a local Pastor. My young wife and I decided it was time to start our family. We had bought a nice home with the money we had saved, and was doing well. Pastor Davis hesitated, looking away as if he was remembering something that was really paining him from the past. Clearing his throat, Pastor Davis continued with his story. "For three years after our return from the mission field, life had taken off at a fast pace for us. Life was good. Everything we had prayed for, and worked towards was happening. When Daisy became pregnant with our first child, I was ecstatic. We had a beautiful home, and I had a job as Senior Pastor of one of the largest-growing churches at the age of twenty-seven. It appeared as if we were living a fairy tale." Pastor Davis hesitated again in his conversation. Paul asked him to continue. It was as if Paul knew that his peace would come as Pastor Davis revealed more of his past to him. Paul began to hold his breath in anticipation as Pastor Davis began to talk again. " It was February. Daisy pregnancy was going smoothly, no complications. I had received a call from one of my deacons of the church, stating that his wife was in labor, and his car would not start. He needed a ride to get her to the hospital. The deacon and I was close friends. We grew up together, and served in the mission field together also. I told Daisy what was happening. She wanted to accompanying me to take them to the hospital, because it was the deacon's wife first pregnancy also and her best friend. As they were best friends. i gave in to her plea. I didn't want her to go because of the bad weather, but she talked me into letting her have her way as usual. I bundled her up, and reluctantly helped her into the car. The roads were very slippery in places. A lot of snow had fallen the day before, and had not been completely cleared. It took at least an hour to get to the deacon house, which was only five miles away. We all bundled into the car, and started the slow drive to the hospital. As we approached the bridge which was only three blocks from the hospital. The car began to lose traction and slide. Daisy was in the back seat when we started out. The deacon was in the front with me, and his wife was in the back seat with Daisy. She was in a lot of pain. Daisy was too large to put the seat belt around her waist, and she was in the back seat with the deacon wife, but when the deacon wife started to need help from her husband, Daisy had to sit in the front seat with me. giving them room in case the baby came. The car lost all traction on the road, sliding into a tree. The impact threw my wife Daisy and our unborn child through the windshield. Just as you have lost, everything that mattered to me disappeared that day. My dreams, my joy, my very ambitions to live just faded away. I felt as if the God I and Daisy had served with all of our hearts had just played a trick on us. I became numb and traumatized. I just stopped breathing, and for the next ten years, I was a dead man walking. I turned my back on God because I felt that he had turned his back on me, so why would I keep serving a God that took everything I had from me?" Paul looking at Pastor Davis felt so relief for the first time since getting the news of his family demise. Paul, humbly ask Pastor Davis, "what happened to you while you were out there in the world? and how did you find your way back to where you are now?" Pastor Davis knows that his answer to Paul has to be seasoned with grace, and wisdom, as the Holy Spirit leads him. He prays for that wisdom now. When Angela returned to the living room, she was confronted with Paul weeping on Pastor Davis shoulder. Angela quietly backed out of the room. Thanking God for little miracles that came in strange and bizarre ways. Angela would never have believed, that God would use Pastor Davis to help save her son again, as he is doing now.

CHAPTER 5

These last three years after John's death. Angela has made the trip back to London along. Her sons always too busy to accompany her was their explanations. Dressed in this lovely gold suit with matching hat and black gloves, trimmed in gold, and draped in a black velvet cape jacket that John had bought for her on their last trip to London on their thirtieth-year anniversary. The weather was brisk this time of the year in London. As Angela approached John's grave, all of her emotions seemed to gather in her chest. Knowing that this might be her last trip, because her health was declining fast, unless she received a bone marrow transplant. and Angela knew that was almost impossible with what she knew. Spreading the small blanket on the grass beside his grave. Angela slid to her knees calling out John's name, as tears of loneliness, frustration, and pain took over her body. The passersby visiting in the cemetery casts glances of concern her way, but didn't invade her privacy. Angela began to confess to John all that had happened this year. The pain and terror of losing Mary and their grandsons, The condition of their son Paul after the murder of his family, and Peter's divorce. Moving here to London with their only granddaughter. Then quietly Angela began to tell John of her medical condition and the need to find Pastor Davis for help. Angela sat with her shoulder leaning against Johns Head stone and went back in time to that day when everything just fell apart. Angela pulled the small blanket around herself, leaning her head against John's head stone, and began unraveling their life to him for the past four years since his death. Paul was not happy with the idea of a visit from his mother and brother at this time of the morning. Even though it was his day off, and Saturday. Paul had just spent most of the night sitting in a bar drinking into the wee hour of this morning, with the woman bartender sending him home, by not serving him any more alcohol. Paul looking out of his front window sees his mother and Peter walking towards his front door. Paul opens the door before they could ring the doorbell. "Come in family." Paul walks into the emergency room waiting area, with a stethoscope around his neck. Peter and Pastor Davis stands up when Paul enters. Paul's face was tired and drawn. Peter rushes up to Paul, searching for answers from his brother. As to what caused their mother to become unconscious after she started convulsing, and bleeding from her mouth and nose back at the house. Paul asked them to follow him to a more private area to talk. Paul explains to them that Angela blood was tested, and found to have a rare form of Leukemia that had caused her to bleed and convulse. It appears that their mother has been sick for quite a few years, even when their father was alive. It seems that he even knew about her sickness, but for some reason they kept it a secret. Privately treating her without the boy's knowledge. Paul could not understand why their parents would keep such a secret from them, when they could possibly save their mother life with their bone marrow. Paul being a physician had to get to the bottom of this. Peter tells his brother that he wants to see their mother. After they leaves the room, Pastor Davis drops to his knees, putting his hands on his head in pure frustration and disbelief. Asking God once again to forgive him, Angela, and John for what is about to happen with this family again after so many years. Pastor Davis knows that changes are about to come in the lives of this family. But he believes that God will work everything out for their good. After releasing all of her pent-up emotions upon Johns grave, Angela still talking to him, began to pull imaginary weeds from around Johns immaculate kept grave site. Deep in conversation, she didn't notice that it had begun to get dark.

Angela rising from her sifting position on the blanket beside John's grave, brushing her dress, continued her one-way conversation with John. "Honey, I think I need to get back to the hotel before it gets to dark. I will visit you again tomorrow around noon. Our son Peter, has invited me over in the evening, to spend some time with them at their new home, before my early morning flight back to the States. At least I can spend part of this visit with our granddaughter. This evening after such a long time. I get to see the look on little Noni's face as she opens the gifts I got her. Peter promised me that they would start visiting you since they now live here in London. maybe after I join you here, they will find it in their hearts to forgive us for the things we did for the sake of love." Angela shaking the blanket, and folding it, leaned down and kissed John head marker. "I love you darling, always will. See you tomorrow as planned. Good night love." Angela turned and exited the cemetery entrance. Walking the two blocks back to her hotel head down deep in thought.

CHAPTER 6

The trains are packed tonight. Being the holiday season, Gigi can hardly breathe or wiggle, as she is being pressed up against so many strangers' bodies. Her train finally come to a screeching stop, and the doors open, spilling its passengers out onto the platforms. Oh! to smell fresh air, and move her body freely is a defining moment for Gigi as she hurries along the train station platform, leading up the steps to London Court, and then the six blocks to her now quiet and lonely townhouse. Pulling her coat and scarf closer to her body to protect her from the late evening crisp air. The weather is beginning to turn colder, only a week from Marks tragic death in the military three years ago. Here in London, holiday decorations are up everywhere. The court yard in the center of the town square was lit up with lights and all colors of ribbons, garlands, and candy canes decorations. They bought their townhouse near the square four and a half years ago. Now she missed the fun of it with Mark, and the rest of the town square community. Gigi walking, began to reminisce about her past life with Mark. Gigi knew that she shouldn't let her mind take her back, but every time she got lonely, she would find solace in hiding in her past memories of the love she had shared with Mark. The love of her life. Mark was snatched away from her so suddenly and too soon. leaving her with bittersweet memories that constantly invaded her every waking and sometimes sleeping hours. When pain came to her heart, she would use those past memories of Mark as a comfort blanket. Gigi, pulling her winter scarf closer around her neck, drifted back into her past memories, as she walked the remaining blocks toward home. The New Year party, she and the other five wives had planned for their spouses, kept them busy, as the men readied themselves for their deployment to the Gulf again. Their unit as Army pilots. Would be gone at least another six months. Gigi and Mark had been arguing all that evening, concerning small insignificant things. Gigi knew she was nitpicking with Mark, because of her feelings of uneasiness with this deployment. Mark had gone on many deployments before, in the seven years of his service. But for some reason she just couldn't explain, this one was different. Mark sisters was always trying to assure her, that Mark would be ok. Mark and the girl's parents, was killed in a plane crash four years ago. Leaving Mark and I, to care for a set of fourteen-year-old girls. We were just married a year. Had no children of our own as of yet. So, this was a challenge for me, being the young spouse of an active duty military pilot, who was deployed six to eight months out of a year. I had to learn quickly how to be a parent. Gigi enjoyed the company of two rambunctious teenagers, but there was something different, going on in her spirit this time. Gigi just couldn't get a grip on her emotions, they were all over the place, and she was constantly finding something to fight with Mark about. The New Year's party, she and the wives had planned for the men, turned out beautiful. Family and friends gathered, not knowing that this would be their last gathering for such a joyous occasion. They had planned to start their family, as soon as Mark returned from this deployment. The girls would be going to the United States, to finish their education. Marks mother's sister, was dean at Yale University. Which their mother was an alumnus. Gigi could see herself and Mark, strolling through London Park, with their small terrier dog she named honey, and pushing their new born baby. To them, the sex of their baby didn't matter, as long as the baby was healthy. Coming out of her dreaming of the past, she began to wonder what will she do with herself now that Mark is gone, and the girls are living in America with their mother's family. Sighing and looking around her, Gigi saw that she was corning up to her neighbor and friend Levy pastry and coffee shop. Her shop was only a block from their townhouse square. Levy would be closing her shop in another hour. Maybe they could walk home together, with Levy living next to her. Gigi enters the pastry shop, with the little bell jingling over the door alerting Levy. She is busy serving a man and a small girl at one of the tables. Gigi smiles and sit at the counter, observing and listening, as the child chatters to the man about how excited she is, about a new house, and some other conversation she could not understand. The man sat appearing captivated with the child's conversation, smiling all the time as she chattered. Levy turns to the counter, and waves for her to join them at the table. Gigi looking around, and seeing that they are the only people in the pastry shop, slides from her seat at the counter, and walks over to the table. Levy introduces Gigi to the man and the little girl. The man stands up as she approaches the table with his hand extended and smiling. The little girl looks at her with her head turned slightly to the side with curiosity. Levy introduces the man as Peter Mason, and his four-year-old daughter Noni Mason. They have just moved to London. Peter is starting a new company, and just bought a townhouse in their community. Gigi shakes Peter Mason hand as she welcomes him and his daughter to London. Sitting back at the counter, after refusing the invitation to join the father and child at their table, Gigi finds herself sneaking peeps at the stranger in deep conversation and laughter with his daughter. She wonders, where is his wife, and why is he here this time of the night, eating alone with a four-year-old in tow? As she waits four Levy to close shop, she finds her thoughts on the handsome man and little girl sitting at the corner table across from her. Like her, he is also wondering, What's her story? Peter and Noni are happy to be living in their new home in London. Noni miss's grandpa and Nanny Janie the housekeeper, that took care of her, when she lived with her mother and grandpa back in the States. Noni missed the girls talks she had with the housekeeper nanny Janie. Nights when she felt lonely and scared. Noni didn't miss that big old scary mansion. Nanny Janie would let her sneak into her room to sleep, when her mother was not around. Which was often. Noni often wondered what happen to cause Nanny Janie to leave without saying goodbye to her. She really missed her a lot. Nanny Janie would help her with things she couldn't figure out by herself. And as Nanny Janie called her daddy, "being a boy man" as Nanny Janie would tell her, "They just didn't understand them, being girls and all." Nanny Janie said "Boys was just like that." Nanny Janie was from Alabama. and she talked really slow. But Noni understood everything she said to her. Not like her mother, who only screamed at her, and was angry all the time. Noni, Looking around smiling as she played, loved the smaller beautiful home her father had bought them. Which was not scary, like grandpa big old dark mansion back in New York. Looking up, from the many toys that her grandma Angela had brought her before she left, going back to the States. Giggling as her father Peter walked into her room with a large box in his arms. filled with more toys from grandpa back in New York. Peter business is coming along well. Noni has just finished talking to grandma Angela back in the United States. They would be visiting grandmother in the States after the holidays season. For grandmother was getting medical treatments she needed to get well. Noni told her father she missed her nanny and friend Janie, and would he find her when they returned to visit New York. He promised her he would do just that. Angela told Peter that Paul was back in his meetings at the church with Pastor Davis, and he returned to work at the hospital. And was busy working to find a cure for her leukemia. All this seemed to keep his mind occupied for now. Peter did not tell his mother, but he and Paul had already discussed that they both would be tested for bone marrow compatibility after the holidays in a week time. They didn't want to put more stress on Angela, so they would do the tests without her knowledge. Peter wonders when the trial is coming up. He stops what he's doing, and calls Taylor for any new information. Hanging up the telephone, after her short and brief talk with Peter concerning the trial, has left Taylor in a bad mood. She didn't want to be the one that informed the family of the death of the man accused of murdering his brother family. The young man had gotten into a fight with another inmate, and was killed. Not wanting to be put in a position of conversation, concerning Paul about his deceased family. She told Peter to call Attorney Roberts, who was prosecuting the case. Taking a deep breath and exhaling, Taylor drops her head, looking into snowflakes eyes, which was fasten intently upon her as to say, who are you?... Taylor has finally met a man that was all about business and career. And that was all she was interested in when it came to men now. After so many years, why did she have to come back to New York. She should have stayed in Japan. Taylor sighing, lets her mind take her back in time Taylor had never been this happy. Just to think about the first glimpse of Paul as he comes through the airport terminal gate was making her nervous with excitement. Thinking back, it has been eight years ago when they kissed goodbye. With Paul boarding the plane headed to America to attend medical school, after his summer vacation in London where they had met. The first four years they stayed in constant touch, with Paul coming to visit for her four-year graduation. Writing and frequent calls, talking about the life they would build after Paul's finishing medical school. With Taylor being a lawyer, and moving to the States, they could build the perfect family and career. The last year of medical school, Paul letters and phone calls began to taper off. When Taylor would call him, he would be too busy, and tell her that he would call her back, but his return calls became less frequent. Taylor also notice that Paul's voice seemed agitated, and not warm towards her as before. He would always tell her that he loved her. But he stopped saying anything concerning love towards her. Then it happened. Paul's letters and calls just stopped. Taylor called Paul, but his call from her went to voice mail. So she wrote him, but he never wrote back. So, after a while Taylor just stopped writing to Paul. While waiting for their connecting flight. Taylor fathers phone rings. IYs a call from Paul's mother Angela, saying that John would not be able to pick her father up from the Airport, for he had fallen from the church balcony stairs, suffering a massive heart attack. Taylor's father a heart specialist. Moved to America several years ago. Her father was now head of The American Heart Association, and living in New York. Taylor and Paul's fathers had been childhood friends. Paul's father John had developed some heart issues that her father was consulting him with, and continued to until! Paul's father's death. Paul's father was schedule to pick him up from the airport. After the fall, Angela called Paul and asked him to pick John's friend up and bring him to the hospital. Taylor didn't know this until! the call came to her father from Angela in flight from London. Now Taylor was standing in line at the terminal. Waiting for the first sight of Paul, whom she had not laid eyes on in eight years. Her heart was doing flip-flops in her chest. Even though she knew what had happened years ago. She knew that she had been replaced in Paul's heart by another woman that he married, and made the life that the two of them had planned out together. Taylor still couldn't quieten her heart. After so many years, the very mention of his name moved her to anxiety. Taylor privately wondered if Paul would be as excited to see her as she was to see him? Even though he didn't know that she was arriving with her father. Taylor was coming to New York for a business meeting, with Mr. Petersen New York branch law firm, for the first visit, as one of their senior partners. The flight from London was announced to arrive earlier than scheduled. The passengers began emerging through the passenger arrival gate. Taylor saw Paul walking towards them, Paul turned his head smiling at the woman holding his hand, and had her other hand resting on a very pregnant abdomen. Taylor knew then, that chapter of her life was closed. Taylor spent the next hour just sitting in her bedroom, away from the noise and traffic of her family and friends. Her toy poodle snowflakes, sat quietly beside her on the bay window sill, overlooking the now frozen lake. Taylor had just celebrated her thirty-eight birthday, and here she was being offered one of the greatest opportunities of her life time. After finishing law school, and being dumped by Paul. Taylor mind made up to put everything she had into building her law career for the next ten years. Determined not to ever let her heart rule her again. The position as a senior law partner, and an executive officer, of one of the largest companies in the world. The company headquarters in New York, Washington D.C. London, and Tokyo Japan. Just what she needs, some space to get far away from New York, and Paul right now. How she was offered the position was just mind blowing to her. Taylor leaned back on the cushion of the window seat with tongue in cheek, letting her mind drift back to when she first met Mr. Petersen. The business and legal mogul of that corporate empire. Taylor was coercing by her best friend to accompany her to a dinner party, because she didn't want to go alone. Taylor owed her friend a favor, so she attended the dinner party with her. Mr. Petersen was the honored guest of the dinner. And her best friend was the fiancé of the guest only son, whom they would meet there with his father. Taylor found herself sitting at the table, with one of the riches and powerful men in the corporate world. Also, her best friend father in law to be. Taylor had no personal interest in the man, except to further her career, which she worked as hard as any man for. Always using her head, and not her heart or body, to get what she wanted. Mr. Petersen was spearheading a serious deal with one of the dinner guests, and Taylor overheard the conversation between the two parties. Not wanting to appear inappropriate, when the other guest excused himself for a break. Taylor advised Mr. Petersen, that the deal he was about to make with the other guest was not profitable for him in the long run. How by accident, that first meeting triggered so many fast changes, that led to her life being transformed into the woman who is now a total stranger, even to herself. This case with Paul family is one that she does not want to be involved in. She knows that all eyes are looking at her to be the lead prosecutor on this case, but her emotions and heart would not do Paul the justice he needs for his family closure.

Taylor father wants her to take the case as prosecutor, because of his loyalty to Paul's deceased father and friend. Shaking her head, No! Taylor turns and walks away from the window overlooking the lake, reaching over to the window sill, and reclaiming the Novella "Mercy Speaks," that she had been reading before the phone call from Peter. Calling snowflakes, and thinking. "I will leave that headache for another day." Taylor heads to bed, with a good book to read, as she and snowflakes exits the room.

SHORT STORY #1

The Five Heartbeats

CHAPTER 1

The weather was brisk at this time of the year in Seattle. Jessica had just closed the door to her office, and gathered her coat collar closer to her neck. Passing the security officer of their law firm building in the lobby, Jessica smiles at him as she approaches. "Hi Fred, I think I'll walk home instead of driving, it's just a couple of blocks, and I need the fresh air to clear my head from today. See you tomorrow." "Goodnight Miss Jessica, bundle up, its cold outside tonight." "Will do Fred." Fred tips his security cap at Jessica, as she walks away, exiting the entrance door of the law building to the street. The walk turned out to be just what she needed. The streets were busy with people. Along the sidewalks were many restaurants, movie theaters, and retailers. Jessica had no one or family here to spend this kind of personal activity with. Ever since her best friend and boss Cory Booker decided to get married, climbing the social ladder of his family wealth. Jessica became just one of the junior law clerks in the Corporate Law Firm of Cory Booker and Associates. Back in Hawaii, Cory finds himself alone. Standing on the now lonely and deserted beach. Everyone has packed up and left the private island that was booked for their wedding. Cory wondered what happened? His newly wedded wife, just got on their private plane with her angry parents, without even looking back at him. Cory pulling his bow tie from around his neck, drops to the sand sobbing, with his hands lifted towards the heavens, and cried out "oh God what did I do so bad that everyone deserted me here?" As Jessica entered the office the next morning. She is met by Cynthia, one of the office laws clerks. Grabbing Jessica by the arm, and pulling her into a vacant break room. Closing the door. "Did you hear what happen to our boss on his wedding? Jessica staring back at her. "No Cynthia, what are you talking about?" Cynthia looking around to make sure no one is within the area, begins to fill Jessica in on Cory's situation. The knock came loud, and insistent at Cory's door. Cory hiding out in his hotel pent house, is not answering his cell phone calls, had Jessica, Cory's employee and best friend worried. They had been best friends all of their childhood up until adults. No one knew them better than each other. Her father was the butler, and personal assistant to Cory's father for twenty-five years. He met and married Cory's mother companion and personal assistant. Jessica mother had died giving birth to her, so she was raised up in the estate household with Cory. Cory is seven years older than Jessica. Jessica was always under foot of Cory. Cory treated her like his younger sister, and would not let his friends disrespect Jessica because of her birth and status. Cory attended the finest Private schools of his family dynasty. Studying and mastered Corporate law and finance. Cory was his father's only child. His father had no living siblings, so Cory inherited the bulk of his fathers and mother estates worth billions. that came with a successful law firm after his father untimely accidental death. Jessica attended public schools, and eventually college, obtaining a law degree. Was employed as a junior law clerk at Cory and Booker Associates law firm. Jessica father was retired from employment at Booker estate after the death of Cory's father, and given a modest home and monthly stipend for his service to Mr. Booker Sr. Jessica remained loyal to Cory despite their social and economic differences. Cory was now her boss and she respected that. Not invading on his privacy. Because of their once closeness as children, and young adults. Before Cory announced his engagement and wedding, Jessica thought she had privy to Cory personal and sometimes business lifestyle. Everything appeared fine between them until! that unfaithful day Cory called a staff meeting. Announcing his engagement to Jocita Wells, a wealthy socialite. Jessica was privately shocked by the public announcement. Because up until] then, they had shared everything she thought with each other. Anyone Cory dated; he would run them through her observations first. It appears his feeling for Jocita Wells, he kept away from her. Jocita was a snobbish, and rich socialite. The daughter of a business friend of Cory's late father. Now Jessica is standing in an uncomfortable position in front of Cory Booker door, knocking, trying to get back into his world. To save him from his mess he has created in his life, and his company. Jessica smelled a rat when it came to Jocita and her family. Jessica always to the rescue of Cory Booker she thought, as she continued to pound on his penthouse door, calling his name. Cory awaken to the pounding in his head, along with another pounding at his front door. Sat up holding his head, then stumbling to the front door, jerks it open, yelling at a blurry figure standing in front of him to go away. Cory tries to slam the door shut, but not before Jessica pushes past him into the apartment. With that stem look of determination upon her face, which he hadn't seen in a long time. Leaving Cory staggering back to the couch, after closing the front door quietly. For his head is pounding. Jessica goes into the bathroom cabinets, finds some aspirin, and a glass of water, returning, hands them to Cory. After taking the aspirins and drinking the water, Cory settles back upon the couch rubbing his head. Jessica tells him she is going to make breakfast while he goes and takes a shower. Frowning and holding her nose, Jessica looks at Cory. "You stink to high heavens my friend." Cory looking down at himself sniffing his shirt. "Gee you are right as usual, butt head." A name Cory called her starting when she was three years old, butting him in the knees, and following him around the estate. It's been a while since I've heard that name." Jessica turns and walks into the kitchen, leaving a quiet Cory sitting on the couch. He smiles then gets up, and heads towards the bathroom. A long shower followed by the cheese egg omelet, fruit and three cups of black coffee. Served to him by Jessica was just what he needed after the last five days of binge drinking. Now dressed in a fresh dark suit, and nice red tie that Jessica had choose and laid out for him before tiding up his place, and leaving for the office herself. Whistling, Cory grabs his briefcase and car keys, thinking it's about time he goes and face all the problems waiting for him at the office. Then chase down the mess of a marriage he just got himself into. Cory, getting off the 6th floor elevator at Cory and Booker Law Firm, was surprise, that he was not bombarded by nosey employees as to his recent predicament. Which he was sure has gotten back to the law firm conceding his marriage situation. What Cory didn't know was that Jessica had called a quick staff meeting, and informed them of the situation, asking them to keep closed mouths concerning their boss's marriage. They all agreed, and conspired with her to do just that. Giving their boss room to sort out his recent problems. No one at the firm liked Jocita Wells and her snobbish family anyways.

CHAPTER 2

There was something about today that Jessica just couldn't put her finger on. Dressing for work this morning was like moving in slow motion. Her mind would not let her move any faster. Ever since Cory got involved with Jocita, he had started to slack off with his clients, leaving a lot of his follow-up appointments, and business meetings with the new guy Winton. There was something about that guy that rubbed Jessica the wrong way. He just didn't sit right in her spirit, she always had a nose for trouble when she saw it, and this guy along with Jocita Wells smelled like trouble. This Guy Winton was just to smooth, and all over the place with the clients, which Cory should have more control of his business deals. This guy was acting like he was a partner at Cory and Booker, instead of a new junior law clerk. He just had to much legal access to the clients, and business of the law firm. When she got a chance, she would bring it to the attention of Cory concerning the security of the firm. Jessica didn't have the assess this new guy had, and she had been with Cory and Booker all her life. Yes, Cory had to get control of his business as well as control of his personal life again. Getting off the elevator, and walking towards her office seemed to quiet this morning. Where was everyone? Coming around the comer, Jessica was met by loud cheering of "happy birthday Jessica." and blowing of paper horns, and balloons popping. Her office friends, the five heartbeats they called themselves; because the law office would come to an abrupt stop without the five law clerks. Cynthia and Megan were holding a large pink candle lit cake. Jessica was so surprised. She had no idea that the office staff liked her this much, to remember her birthday, which she seemed to have forgotten. Wiping her eyes of joyful tears, Jessica hugged and thanked everyone of them. "Thank you all for being so kind to me. You all remembered my birthday. Which I forgot was today." Megan smiling as they put the cake down on the nicely decorated table filled with cards and surrounded by hanging balloons. "You must be kidding girl; how could we forget your birthday after the big bonus checks you fought for us to receive last month. How do you think we paid for this party?"What's going on here?" Jessica turning towards the voice, as staff looks on being confronted by Mr. Winton. "Mr. Winton it's my birthday, and the staff surprised me. Would you like to join us in this small celebration? "No Miss Jessica, I think you all need to do that on your own time, and not the company time. That's not what you are getting paid to do. Good day Miss Jessica. Now everyone needs to get back to work." Abruptly turning his back on everyone Mr. Winton exited the room. At 3:15pm, a meeting of the office staff was announced by Mr. Winton. Mr. Cory Booker would be down to meet with his staff concerning changes within the company All staff was to be present. With the staff present in the staff board room, in walks Mr. Booker accompanied by Mr. Winton and two senior law partners. At the end of the meeting, Jessica and the rest of the staff had decided to take her birthday celebration to their little hide out spot. A small bar two blocks away from their office. Owned by Megan's husband. There they could discuss secretly and quietly amongst themselves what just transpired here, out of ear shot of Mr. Winton and other office snoops. After the company was closed for the day, and all the staff had left. Cory was very upset with himself, that he totally forgot Jessica birthday for the first time in their lives. He was floored when he walked into the staff office, and saw the happy birthday Jessica banner hanging over the door. And the half eaten pretty pink cake that she loved on her birthday since she was one year old. Sitting now with his head hung low behind his desk in his office, Cory knows that he has to do something over the top to win favor back in Jessica eyes. Sitting in their favorite spot in the back of Jack's Bar and grill, was Jessica, Megan, Cynthia, Trent, and Shelton. The five heartbeats as they called themselves of the Cory Booker and Associates law firm. They considered themselves the pulse of the law firm. Nothing moved without their imputes. They knew that as law clerks within the firm, their jobs were very important. They kept everything going smoothly and on legal time within the firm. They were the watch dogs of the firm. Cory thank all of them for jobs well done while he was absent. Stating that Mr. Winton had reported that we were up to date with all of our cases. Mr. Winton was being considered to chair a new position within the company in a few months. We as law clerks were to work closely with him to continue get the jobs done. Now the five heartbeats had their heads together, because not only did Jessica smell a rat, but the rest of them had begun too, when it came to Mr. Winton. They decided that they had to start doing some background digging of their own, to get all the goods on Mr. Winton. They have a feeling that he was hiding something. And as law clerks they would dig and find the goods on him. So, they called in one of their old partners to help flush out the stink on Mr. Winton. Jessica, had enjoyed the birthday celebration night out, with her friends from the office. It was a Friday night, so they stayed late. Partying, and everyone drinking and having fun, even though she was not a drinker. They had her all non-alcoholic wind up. Back in her small apartment walk up flat. She was not sleepy, and here she was after midnight, on a Friday night restless. Heading to the kitchen to make her a cup of warm milk, thinking that's what her father uses to give her, when she could not sleep as a child. Was that her door bell ringing? Opening her door, to find Cory leaning against the wall. Dressed in a white tux, white top hat and white gloves. Holding a pink lit cake with a big grin on his face. Standing beside a white limousine with an open rear door, was the limo driver. Holding a large vase of pink roses. And as I already knew, a bottle of nonalcoholic champagne. Jessica reaches out grabs Cory by his lapel, and pulls him into her flat. Then urges the limo driver to come in to. The limo driver enters, arranges the vase of flowers on the dining room table with the bottle of champagne, tips his hat and excuses himself. Cory apologize for forgetting her birthday for the first time in their lives. Jessica thanks him for the grand gesture of tonight. Laughing that only Cory could pull something off as he just did with her. Cory talked Jessica into dressing, and going for a ride around the City of Seattle in the limo, as they ate cake and drunk more nonalcoholic champagne. Cory wondered if anyone ever got drunk on that stuff.

CHAPTER 3

Cory woke up to someone kissing him. Thinking of pink cake and champagne, Cory leans in to the kiss calling Jessica name. The sting of a slap brings him wide awake. Standing over him with flashing eyes is Jocita. Jumping out of the bed, Cory rubbing his face, asks Jocita how did she get into his apartment. Jocita reminds Cory that she is his wife, and can come and go as she pleases. Letting Cory know that the bellhop let her in, because she now lives here. Cory grabbing her by the arm, leads her to the couch demanding explanations, as to why she and her parents left the Island the way they did. And where has she been for the last two months. Cory told her that since he could not fund her, and she didn't communicate with him as to her whereabouts. He had started legal proceedings to annul the marriage. Jocita told Cory that her best friend, and maid of honor, told her parents that he had forced himself upon her, the day before our wedding. That she was to embarrassed, and afraid to tell anyone. Until after the wedding the next day. Jocita said her parents made her leave the Island with them that night. Taking the wedding party with them from the Island, sending all of our guest's bogus excuses. Jocita said her parents would not let her talk to him, and took her out of the country to Spain their home. She said that when she found out that she was pregnant, her best friend came clean, telling her and her parents that she had lied on him. because she was jealous of their marriage. Jocita parents then put her on a plane back to the United States, and to her husband. Telling her to let him know, that they are so sorry for what happened. Cory sat on the couch in disbelief at what he is hearing from Jocita. His life was turned upside down in one day. And just when he thought he was finally getting it righted again, Jocita shows up with a story, out of a horror novel, and pregnant as well, of one wedding night. Cory holding his now hurting head, can't believe what a mess he has gotten himself in. If his father was alive right now, this would kill him all over again. Jocita settles right in, like she had never been gone. She calls her parents, telling them that we are together and happy with the baby coming. She has already rearranged the pent house apartment. Hired a maid, a cook, and chauffeur. Even though I don't see any need for them. She is only two months pregnant. I don't see much of her, because she spends them out with her socialite friends. I spend most of my waking time at the office to avoid her. Back at the office I explain to Jessica the situation of Jocita coming back pregnant after two months. Jessica appears to keep her feelings well hidden from me. But after the night of her birthday, I realized that there's something more between Jessica and I, than growing up together, and now as employer and employee, my waking and sometimes sleeping hours are filled with Jessica and not Jocita. I spend more time at the office and calling Jessica to make small talk than being home talking to Jocita. Jessica hangs the phone up after a call from the old friend of her father that use to be employed by Cory's father for many years as a private investigator. He called Jessica to inform her that a certain Mr. Winton, has been spotted keeping company at a certain hotel, with a woman name Jocita Wells. They have been meeting there every day, for a couple of hours. for the two weeks of her return to the United States. At a certain time of the evening, and weekends. The private Investigator has photos of them kissing, hugging and making body contact on the balcony. The hotel room is checked out in Jocita Wells name. Jessica told him to get as much information as he could before they expose them to Cory. Now Jessica is believing that the baby Jocita is carrying is Mr. Winton, instead of Cory's. It's strange that Mr. Winton was hired around the same time that Jocita and her family came into Cory's life. They were always just distant business friends of Cory's father in the past. Even though Jocita knew Cory, she never made a pass at him until the death of Cory's father. Very strange indeed. Cory had called Jessica to his office concerning the bar exam which she was preparing to take. While they were leaning over the application discussing it, Jocita barges her way into Cory office, despite his secretary disapproval trying to announce her presence. Eyes flashing, and loudly accusing Cory of not coming home, because of, "This thing! Is this why you stay late at the officer Cory anger flares up at Jocita, and her rudeness to his staff. "Excuse me Jessica, while I talk to my wife for a minute." Jessica picks up the application from Cory desk and leaves the room. Closing the office door behind her. She and Cory's secretary exchanges, that look. As Jessica passes her desk on her way back to her office. A few minutes later, Jocita comes out of Cory's Office walking fast, with her head down as she passes his secretary's desk. Cory secretary eyes follow her out the door, wondering what he could have said to her, that got that kind of response.

CHAPTER 4

The next morning when Jessica arrived at work, the office was buzzing. It appears that just as Mr. Winton came, he also left. The explanation he gave, was that his mother had fallen seriously ill, and he being the only child, had to go back to Spain to take care of her. No one in the office knew that he came from Spain. His resume was sent from Cory fathers friend law office, highly recommending Mr. Winton for the job vacancy. What a coincident. A notice had just come down to the law clerks office from Mr. Cory Booker and Associates law firm. That the position for Mr. Winton position, and the new management position that he was being considered for, would be hired from within their law clerks pool of employees. These positions would remain open until! someone takes and pass the bar exam within the present law clerks. Everyone was excited over the sudden absent of Mr. Winton, and the possibility of job advancements in their office. Cory Booker secretary arrived, requesting that Jessica and the other four law clerks staff members accompany her back to Mr. Booker office. Everyone became quiet, wondering what had happen for their boss to send his secretary to demand their presence in his office. A knock came on Cory Booker's office door. "Enter." Jessica and the other staff quietly walk into the office. Looking around not knowing what to expect. "Close the door behind you." Cory looking calmly at them. "Is there something you five needs to discuss with me?" Jessica, looking at the fear that has come upon the others and their hesitation. clears her throat. "May I speak alone with you. Please?" Cory stares at her for a moment. "Ok you all may leave." They all glances at Jessica with looks of regret, as they leave the office, closing the door behind them. "Sit down Jessica, and start from the beginning, don't leave anything out, our future depends upon what you have to say here today." Jessica dropping her head, began to lay out everything that had happened. Leaving nothing unsaid, even her feelings for him all the years. She knew that with everything out in the open, maybe Cory could salvage what's left of his personal life, and business before that woman Jocita and her family destroyed it and him. As usual, she would sacrifice her feelings, career and happiness for him. She has loved Cory from the age of one year old, when he wiped her snotty nose and tears, every time she hurt and cried, he was always there for her. Maybe it was time for her to move on. Creating a life for herself outside of Cory Booker. He didn't need her watching over him, protecting him. He was a grown man. Married the woman he wanted as his companion and mother of his children. Even if that woman had other motives, Cory chose her as his wife. Jocita was not right for Cory, but he chose her. Cory saw her only as a friend and employee. It was time for her to let go and move on. After Jessica had told Cory everything that they had done trying to protect him and the company. Hiring a private investigator, spying on Jocita and Mr. Winton. Digging into their backgrounds. Finding out that the two were lovers, trying to get their hands-on Cory's law firm as an employee, and Cory estate. By Jocita marriage, and claiming an heir through her pregnancy, which was really Mr. Winton and not Cory. Jessica turned to leave Cory office, asking him to not fire the others for their part in the plotting, which she engaged them to get involved. Because like her, they really were faithful employees. To please let them keep their jobs. She was leaving the company, but please let them stay. As Jessica once again went to open the door, Cory came up behind her, pushing it close again. "Jessica you don't think for one moment that I will let you walk out of my life so freely. Don't you understand by now that I can't survive, and don't want to without you in my life. Not just as my friend and employee, but as my wife, lover, and mother of my children. To share everything, I have been so gifted with, and left by my parents. You have been a part of my life as long as i can remember, and You are not walking out of it now. I know about Mr. Winton and my so-called wife Jocita. I know that they are already married, and are con artists. That's how they got their wealth. They along with Jocita parents, targeted me after my father's death. The investigations is finished, and they are all in police custody. Putting my father's accidental death at the hands of Jocita Father. Trying to get control of my father's company and estate. Then after my father's death, they used their son in law and own daughter to try carrying out the plan of disposing of me too. Leaving Jocita as my widow, and supposedly child. as heir to my fortunes. Then they would live happily afterwards. They have been exposed. You five heartbeats of Cory Booker just helped the officials move the case along quicker. That's the real reason why I called you five up here, was to thank you for looking out for me. Jessica darling, you are the love of my life. You are a permanent fixture in my heart. Our parents would be proud of us about right now. They must have known something we didn't know as children. That fate brought two families together. A servant and his master. That there is something stronger than money that can bond hearts together. The gift of love, when sown in its purest form will never die." Cory Booker, turning Jessica around as she leaned back against the door. Was kissing her hard, as she opens the door to the listening ears, and grinning faces of the other four heartbeats, and a smiling handclapping secretary, sitting at her desk, giving them all the eye over her glasses.

SHORT STORY #2

The son My Father Never had

CHAPTER 1

Pressing my braided hair to my head with shaking hands, I wondered how in the world was I, Jackie Madela going to pull this last one off? Looking back at me in the mirror was a lonely and scared young African American Woman who had played the part of a dead billionaire son Jason Jr. for the last twelve years. Keeping a company alive and prosperous without the board members or office staff ever laying eyes on me. Now with my adopted father dead, and his faithful friend and lawyer Mr. Jonas Sims of sixty years in partnership with him as my only alibi. I wondered how was I going to get myself out of this mess in one piece. Well let me tell you the story of how it started and, twelve years later, a billionaire in my own rights, was standing in the office of two of the riches dead men that once lived. Getting ready to walk into the room of eight executive board members of that company that I've ran those twelve years for those board members. Some of the world's most powerful and riches men still alive. Squaring my shoulders, like my adopted father had taught me when facing a challenge or crises I cleared my throat, pushed my braids back from my face, opened my adopted father's office door leading into the board room, and came to an abrupt halt. Sitting around the Conference table in front of me was eight pairs of eyes hard and cold as steel staring back at me. Clearing my throat gain. I walked into the room, never lowering my eyes from the eight pairs of steel that I was confronted with. Mr. Sims, my adopted fathers' friend and lawyer, smiling as I entered, rose from the conference table addressed the men in greetings. Gentlemen let me introduce you to the heir of Braggs and Goldman's, Ms. Jackie Madela. Aka Jason Goldman Jr. deceased. All eyes remained on Jackie as her lawyer Mr. Sims took his seat. Jackie knew she was the center of attention, as every board member waited for explanations of everything that had just happened. Jackie walking to the penthouse window of Braggs and Goldman's with her back turned to the men in the room began to unravel the events of the past twelve years. subject came easy for me. I didn't do much studying, and passed all of my tests with no trouble. Everything was easy especially math and science. I wanted to become a scientist and worked at NASA one day. I was always daydreaming about building space shuttles. The boys at school teased me, saying girls didn't do that kind of work. I needed to become a teacher or a nurse. Mr. and Mrs. Goldman Sr. had only a son, Jason Jr. who was my age. But he was wild and mean spirited. My mother told me to stay out of his way. Mrs. Goldman, even though she was sick, Jason Jr. would yell at her, and take her money to go do drugs with his friends Mr. Goldman would give him only his weekly allowance and nothing else. which he also used up on drugs. Mr. Goldman began working often from his home office, since Mrs. Goldman became very ill. I would hear him working late into the night on projects. Mr. Goldman Sr. was an automobile builder of luxury cars, which he exported, and sold to luxury automobile dealerships in the United States, and other countries around the world, from Germany. One-night I heard him on the phone, talking to someone about having hundreds of millions of dollars on the line, and it seemed like he was going to lose this deal. Because they could not figure out a combustion formula that they had been working on for almost a year. Their deadline for the delivery of those cars was in two weeks. They had not come up with the proper combustion, to pass the EPA standard for emission control. The cars had to past the emission test to be allowed shipment to other countries for sales. They had hundreds of millions of dollars riding on this deal. Out of my curiosity as usual, I waited until Mr.

Goldman Sr. became exhausted and went to bed. My mother said her prayers, and was down for the head count by ten. The son was out of the house as usual, and Mrs. Goldman was bedridden and had been given her sleeping meds for the night. So, I could have the roam of the house So here I was in Mr. Goldman office, looking at all the charts of automobiles and engine parts, mathematical charting, and scientific formulas that he had spent a year trying to formulate into a working system. I was finally in my world so to speak. These chances don't come often. Making the best of my situation. Locking the office door began to

CHAPTER 2

Jason Goldman Sr. kept writing on the pad in front of him then as quickly erase what he had written. "God damn it!!! I just can't seem to come up out with the right figures this morning." The telephone rings, answering it Mr. Goldman Sr. is heard telling the other party to meet him at the golf resort club house in half an hour I am 17 at the time, living with my mother in the maids quarters of Mr. Goldman estate, because we were thrown out of my mother's brothers house, because my mother prayed and sang to loud. My uncle wife didn't like my mother, so she always found fault in everything my mother did. My uncle told my mother we had to make other living arrangements. So, my mother asked permission of Mrs. Goldman who was very sick at the time, if I could stay with her in the maid quarters. I was old enough to do house work after school, and help Mrs. Goldman. Mrs. Goldman thought that was a very good idea. I didn't like it, but I had no other choice, but to do what I was told by my mother. Everyone at school including my teachers wanted to know what my future plans was after high school. Because it seemed like every subject came easy for me. I didn't do much studying, and passed all of my tests with no trouble. Everything was easy. especially math and science. I wanted to become a scientist and worked at NASA one day. I was always daydreaming about building space shuttles. The boys at school teased me, saying girls didn't do that kind of work. I needed to become a teacher or a nurse. Mr. and Mrs. Goldman Sr. had only a son, Jason Jr. who was my age. But he was wild and mean spirited. My mother told me to stay out of his way. Mrs. Goldman, even though she was sick, Jason Jr. would yell at her, and take her money to go do drugs with his friends Mr. Goldman would give him only his weekly allowance and nothing else. which he also used up on drugs. Mr. Goldman began working often from his home office, since Mrs. Goldman became very ill. I would hear him working late into the night on projects. Mr. Goldman Sr. was an automobile builder of luxury cars, which he exported, and sold to luxury automobile dealerships in the United States, and other countries around the world, from Germany. One-night i heard him on the phone, talking to someone about having hundreds of millions of dollars on the line, and it seemed like he was going to lose this deal. Because they could not figure out a combustion formula that they had been working on for almost a year. Their deadline for the delivery of those cars was in two weeks. They had not come up with the proper combustion, to pass the EPA standard for emission control. The cars had to past the emission test to be allowed shipment to other countries for sales. They had hundreds of millions of dollars riding on this deal. Out of my curiosity as usual, I waited until Mr. Goldman Sr. became exhausted and went to bed. My mother said her prayers, and was down for the head count by ten. The son was out of the house as usual, and Mrs. Goldman was bedridden and had been given her sleeping meds for the night. So, I could have the roam of the house So here I was in Mr. Goldman office, looking at all the charts of automobiles and engine parts, mathematical charting, and scientific formulas that he had spent a year trying to formulate into a working system. I was finally in my world so to speak. These chances don't come often. Making the best of my situation. Locking the office door,' began to investigate my findings. Before i knew it, the car engine parts became alive in my head, and running, math became formulas in my head, and my hands began to chart a mathematical mapping of the mechanical engineering and combustion system. I analyzed all the data, and imputed it on the chart. Mapping the correct combustion and emission control system for the engine. Now all its parts were in perfect working conditions on the charts. They just had to be put together and tested. Before I realized it, the daylight was coming through the windows. I was so glad it was Saturday morning. and not a school day. Because I would have been in so much trouble. I can fake a headache this morning with my mother, to get some much-needed sleep. Hearing people stirring, I slipped out of Mr. Goldman Sr. office and went straight to bed. They could hear Mr. Goldman Sr. hollering all over the house. Everyone came running. Even the gardener heard him, and came to see what was going on. I slept through it all. My mother told me what happen later on, when she came to check on me and my headache. Giving me a strange knowing look, but didn't say or ask me nothing......

To be continued in Novella Series #2 Mercy Speaks....

SHORT STORY #3

A City Called Mothers Arms.

Micah felt like she was losing her balance every time she bent over to make the bed. She hadn't taken the time to eat this morning before leaving for the hotel. Making sure her daughter was up and dressed. The lady Ms. Tamara, the manager back at Mothers Arms sixteen bed women's shelter, a safe house for battered women and children. Ms. Tamara had taken a liken to her and her daughter Milani. She said they reminded her of the relationship she uses to have with her daughter. Ms. Tamara kept an eye on Milani while she worked at the hotel. Ms. Tamara had been a battered woman, and was sympathetic with the women and their children at the shelter. Micah was a quiet young woman of Latin American descent. She and her four-year-old daughter Milani had been moving from city to city.

Standing on the side of highways, thumbing rides from strangers for the last year knowing it was dangerous. Micah decided to settle here in Atlanta Georgia. Micah heard from a distant relative back in New York, that her husband Jonas had been killed in prison. After looking for them Jonas in a rage took the life of her boss Mrs. Mary Mason, and her two boys that was Malini's age. She and Milani had made it all the way down south to Georgia, running away from that crazy husband of hers. The morning they had left New York was the scariest day of her life. Jonas had been on a rage all night. Drinking and doing meth. She had locked herself and Milani up in the bath room, until! Jonas fell into a drunken and meth induced sleep. She then grabbed the money she had been stashing away from her job at the daycare center. Micah packed some clothing, taking the first bus out of New York. It didn't matter where they were going to get away from Jonas, and that gun he was always threatening them with. Micah felt so sorry for what happen to her boss and her children, but she knew that if she hadn't run away, the same thing would have happened to them. She was glad that her fear let up long enough for her to leave. Micah finally could rest, without looking over her shoulders, afraid of seeing her husband angry face even in her dreams.

Micah didn't have time to stand in line for the breakfast this morning before being dropped off at the hotel for work. She could not afford to lose her job. It was her only way of becoming independence of the shelter and being homeless. She was saving every dime to rent a small flat for her and Milani. As her day continued, Micah weakness and dizziness were getting unbearable. She had been told years ago after the birth of Milani that she suffered low blood sugar, and had to eat regular meals to stay healthy. Remembering that an untouched breakfast tray was in one of the rooms she had cleaned. Thinking maybe the kitchen help hadn't removed the tray, Micah open the door, and seeing the breakfast tray intact with the food untouched. Micah being weak and hungry, hurried over to the tray and began eating. Micah interest was so focus on the food that she didn't see the man sitting by the window reading a newspaper. "Young lady, can I help you?" With a piece of toast in her mouth, Micah turned in disbelief, looking in sheer horror into the kindest gray eyes she had ever seen. Micah dropped the piece of toast, as she ran out of the room in total humiliation, at the situation she has gotten herself into. Faced with the possibility of losing her job. Her focus the rest of the day, was on hearing her name being called, by the hotel manager over the intercom. The end of Micah shift came to an end without a call from management. Micah left the hotel with the other women at the end of their shift. The hotel shuttle van arrived daily, to transport the women from the shelter to the hotel for work, and back to the shelter.

Greeting her daughter's Milani smiling face changed the frown on Micah face to a smile. Hugging her daughter small body close to hers. Gave her a more secure and calm feeling. Micah discussed the incident with Tamara, of how she got caught eating from an untouched food tray in one of the hotel rooms by a guest because of her health crisis. Tamara instructed her to be truthful with management if they called her to their office about the incident. Talking to Tamara left Micah feeling better about the incident. Except the embarrassment with the man in the room, that she wished never happened. She wondered what kind of person he thought she was. The incident with the beautiful and scared maid yesterday, was in Anthony thoughts all night and again this morning. He could not forget the look of sheer fright he saw on her beautiful face. He could not get it out of his mind. Why was she so hungry? Did she not have money to buy food, why was she so desperate? Anthony made up his mind that he would get to the root of her problems, if nothing else but to put a smile back on that beautiful face. He knew that he never wanted to see that desperation on her face again if he could help it. Anthony had finished all of his once a year private inspection on fifteen hotels, this one being his last. Pleased with the majority of what he found. Anthony didn't think being on the top five-star hotels list would be a problem for his hotels, Minor discrepancy was found, but nothing management and staffing training could not handle. Anthony took it upon himself to travel to all of the hotels he owned. Once a year for three months to do inspections. He would show up without management knowledge, that way management would be inspired to keep his hotels in top shape year-round. That had been working very well for nine years. Anthony decided that since he was finished with his inspections, it was time for him to relax a little here in Atlanta with a few friends before he goes back to Canada. There was no one back at home to keep him company. Jenny had been dead for five years now, and her memories, no matter how wonderful they were, they were just that. Time seem to gather on you quickly with memories. Anthony found himself needing more than just memories. Jenny will always hold a part of his heart no matter what. Anthony as always, every year after a great inspection of his hotels, he would have a banquet for the staffing, and give bonus checks.

Management was left to prepare the banquet for the staff, using outside services. The hotel staff was not to be involved in the work, they and their immediate family were guests that Saturday night only. To receive their bonus checks which equal another pay check. The hotel staff had to be present at the banquet. This way Anthony got to greet and meet every employee of his once a year as he gave them their bonuses. The word was passed to all the staff about the banquet. All the women at the shelter that worked at the hotel was excited about the extra money and the opportunity to dress up, go out with their family and enjoy. Micah wasn't excited about going to the banquet, she wore the hotel uniforms every day to work, and only had a couple of jeans and tee shirts for everyday wear. Smiling Micah thought the bonus would be the extra money she needed to move them to their apartment. Just one more pay check, she would be able to move them to their own place. Micah help came from Tamara. Calling Micah to her room, she had the most beautiful blue silk dress laid out on her bed that Micah had ever seen. Tamara explained that the dress belonged to her daughter. It was the dress her daughter had worn to her prom, the night before she ran away from home. Leaving only the dress hanging in her closet. The dress was the only thing she had left, to remind her of a daughter she hasn't seen in seven years. Tamara explained why her daughter left home. She got tired of seeing her mother get beat down by her father every day, for the smallest of things. Her daughter begged her to leave for years after every beating, but she was to scared. So, the day after graduation, Tamara daughter left herself, and didn't look back. Tamara wiping tears, picked up the dress handing it to Micah, with a smile told her to go to the banquet, and have enough fun for the both of them. Milani birthday was coming up in a couple of weeks, and Micah had bought her a beautiful little yellow sundress and ribbons from the thrift store across the street. walking the day before, Micah had found a ten-dollar bill on the ground. The dress and ribbons only cost her seven dollars. She knew Milani would love the dress and ribbons. She was to young to care where it was purchased from. That was a blessing in itself as also finding the money. On Saturday evening, the hotel van came to pick up the hotel staff and their families for the banquet. The women and children looked very nice dressed up. Everyone at the shelter went out of their way to make sure that the women and children from Mother's Arm shelter dressed in their finest. The children were having so much fun dressed up. The banquet was in full swinging party mode when they arrived. music and food everywhere, with lovely decorations. The room was very beautiful and festive. The children ran off immediately looking for food. As Micah stood looking around, she was not aware that she was being observed from across the room. Anthony couldn't take his eyes away from the beautiful woman dressed in blue standing across the room from him. He didn't realize that he was holding his breath until one of the managers ask him was, he okay. Then he exhaled with a questionable "yes." The children were having so much fun. Micah told Milani not to eat too much, she might get a tummy ache. Milani rubbing her stomach with a frown told Micah she thinks it's too late for that. The banquet had turned out nicely, everyone had eaten, and danced Now setting down at our tables getting ready to be greeted by our boss and management. Management walked into the room, and behind them walked the most handsome man Micah had seen in a long time. The room lights were dimmed as they entered, but as they came closer into the room, Micah swore she could feel her hair stand up on her head. For right in front of her standing at the podium was the man with the kindest gray eyes staring back at her. "Oh my god." A look of sheer terror came in her eyes again as darkness over took her. Micah could hear her name being called by Milani as she rubbed her mother's face, still calling her name. "Mommy, wake up." Opening her eyes, the faces before her was Milani and the man from the hotel room. Sitting up and looking around, Micah wondered where she was.

It looked like the pent house apartment in the hotel. She always wondered what it looked like inside. Shaking her head. "Be careful my dear, we wouldn't want you to faint again would we. Then i'll have to call the doctor. "Micah still rubbing her head tried to get up, but was pushed back against the couch by a gentle, but firm hand of the man. "Don't try to move to fast, get your balance first." hello, I am Anthony Harpor, the owner of this hotel. I am so sorry that we keep meeting in such disadvantage ways." This time Anthony would have appreciated if she was not looking at him with such fright. People might think of him as a dangerous person. Micah slowly sat up. Apologizing for the incident. Explaining about the emergency medical condition, that caused her to seek out the food that way. Which if not eaten, would cause her to pass out if her blood sugar continued to drop. Anthony listening, was very concerned about her health, just losing his wife a few years ago to health issues. Micah told him that after that episode, she was more careful with her health. Poor Milani was exhausted from all the excitement and drama of the day had fallen asleep on the couch. Anthony smiling down at her, asked Micah if it was ok to put her in the bed, so that she could be more comfortable. Micah looking tenderly with love upon her small daughter, nodded in agreement. After making the child comfortable in the large bed, Anthony turned his attention back to the mother. Sitting again on the couch, Anthony explained to Micah that after she fainted, and the doctor was called. She was given a good bill of health by her, but said that she needed to rest. Anthony brought her up to the pent house to rest and get away from prying eyes. He also made a call to Tamara at the Mother's Arm shelter. Putting her at ease about their situation. Giving Tamara his phone number to the pent house. To call and check up on Micah herself if she wanted to. Micah was uncomfortable with their sleeping arrangements, and ask Anthony where was he sleeping. He told her he had that taken care of, with over 152 beds in the hotel building. He didn't think that would be a problem. Thanking Anthony, and apologizing again for such inconveniences to him. Anthony started to ask Micah questions about her and, her situation in the shelter. Micah stood up saying that she was tired, and didn't want to talk about that tonight. Could that conversation wait for another day? Anthony apologized, excusing himself. "Goodnight Micah, see you in the morning, sleep well." After Anthony left, Micah knew she had to rise early, catching a ride from the hotel shuttle van back to the shelter. She knew she had to get as far away from those kinds, and questioning gray eyes as possible. Rising early that Sunday morning, Micah and Milani rode back to the shelter on the hotel van, without seeing Anthony. Micah knew she would not be schedule to work again until! Tuesday. She was going to move into the kitchenette apartment, being held for her by a friend of Tamara's. The apartment was only a block from the shelter, and Tamara was going to continue watching Milani for her, at the shelter while she worked. After moving their meager belongings into their apartment. Micah thanked Tamara and her friend for what they were doing for her. Wiping her watery eyes with brown hard worked hands, Tamara hugged Micah and Milani to her as she leaves. Tells them they have become the closest feeling of family to her in years. She will miss their company, even though they are only a block away, and see them every day. It's different from living in the same house with them. Now Tamara got Micah and Milani bawling. Micah felt good about herself for the first time in years, even though she was only twenty-nine years old. Her life with Jonas had been a living hell. The abuse had taken a toll on her. She knew that like Tamara's daughter, if she hadn't gotten Milani out of that situation, Milani might have ended up as a runaway, or dead like the children of her boss back in New York. Shaking off the memories from her head, Micah began fixing lunch. She had enough money left over from paying apartment rent, to buy them enough groceries to last another week. She also purchased a small tv from the thrift shop for twelve dollars. So that Milani wouldn't be bored. She so liked watching cartoons at the shelter. for a three-year-old, it kept her entertained. Micah thanked god the apartment came furnished. she only had to purchase some kitchen and bathroom supplies, which Tamara had already supplied for them. The rent was cheap enough for Micah to afford. Tuesday morning Micah returned to work, expecting to thank Anthony for all his help. But as the day progressed, Anthony never appeared. Micah finally asked one of the managers where she could find him. To thank him for helping her after the banquet. The manager told her Anthony had left the day before, headed back to Canada. Micah thank him for his time. Walking down the hotel hallway, Micah wondered what caused him to cut his visit so short. He had told her, he was taking some time off in Atlanta to relax. Micah felt disappointed for some reason. The rest of her week went by quietly and peacefully....

To be continued in...Novella Series #2 Mercy Speaks"
...coming soon...2020...

SHORT STORY #4

The Meeting of Two Worlds

CHAPTER 1

The first glimpse of Rose mother's home land brought joy and anxiety to Rose's heart. Rose's mother had spent hours holding her sweet baby girl on her lap as she grew up in America. Mesmerizing her with stories of her childhood back in the beautiful lands of black gold called Africa. Rose stood at the entrance of the Pan African Airlines plane, as they prepared to unloaded her mother's casket from the storage area into the funeral home transport. Deep in thought, Rose remembered her mother's last words to her. "My sweet daughter, take your mother's body back to her home land, so that i might rest with my ancestors." Rose promised her mother that she would honor her last living wish. Her father did not agree with that decision but it did not change her mind from following through with her mother's wishes. Now standing beside her mother's casket with no familiar face to welcome them. Her heart is beating, telling her to be strong, and finish what you have promised your mother. But Rose's head is saying to her, get a return flight quickly back to America. You have no reason to linger here after your mother's burial. While waiting for clearance, Rose began to reminisce of her mother telling her stories of her childhood her in Africa. rose mother told her that right after secondary school, her parents shipped her off to America. To New York to live with her mother sister to guarantee her education, because she was their only child. Rose mother had her mesmerized with the beautiful stories she would tell her. The wonderful stories of her parents, and the village that they lived in. But as Rose grew up, she would ask her mother why she never visited Africa or took her to visit? The answer would always be the same as years passed. Rose father was American and he had no interest in visiting Africa. He finally separated from my mother, and divorced her, remarrying again. Rose was always sad that they didn't take the time to make connections with my mother's homeland. Rose parents were medical doctors. Always busy working. Rose spent most of her childhood in private boarding school, following the same occupation as her parents. In her youth, when not in school, she was at home along with the house staff. Rose knew that her parents loved her dearly, for she was there only child, and demonstrated it in the only way they knew. They believed in being educated and financially successful.

Rose was brought out of her daydreaming as a blast of Africa's heat hit her in the face, causing her to quickly pull off the shawl from around her shoulders. The weather in New York was cool on their departure. But now her in Africa the heat was swelling and offensive to her first visit. Rose was sweating already, standing at the Pan Africa Airlines exit cargo door, as they unload her mother's remains, and load her casket into the waiting mortuary van for transport to the mortuary facility. Rose looking around could hear her mother's frantic last plea to her. "I beg you child, and while you are there in Africa, take time out to get to know your distant family, land, and culture. Please do this for me your mother." My mother looking intently at me called me closer to her bed side. Handing me a small black book, instructed me to follow it to the T. For in that book was her whole life mapped out for my future. Now I am standing here in her beloved Continent of Africa, with her remains and this little black book trying to follow it to the T.

CHAPTER 2

The Journey

Rose journey lasted six years following her mother's instructions in that little book. From the last time she viewed America from the window of that Pan African Airlines plane, until her flight from Istanbul finally ended at John F. Kennedy Airport New York City. Rose can't wait for her feet to touch America soil again. If people only knew the true gift of having plenty. After spending the last two years of her six-year journey as a medical doctor traveling and working in some of the poorest African countries in the Democratic Republic of Congo, and Central African Republic. Rose fell in love with the people. But after two years of living without the barest personal hygiene essentials, she was more than ready to go home. Rose mother had not visited her home of Africa since she left for America at 19 years of age. But she never forgot her Africa, her parents and family. After coming to America, she mastered her education, and developed the work ethics taught by her parents. Making provision for them back home in Africa until their death, along with providing for her people. my mother being the only child, poured her financial resources into helping educate the youth, and build medical facilities in the poor and isolated areas of Africa. My mother was a humanitarian to her people first, then to the world. This was all written in that little black book for her daughter to follow to the T as she wrote.

Rose, being the dutiful and loving daughter that she was. Followed her mother's instructions, which took her on a six-year journey to fulfill her mother's wishes. Rose mother had made prosperous financial business deals, that left Rose a very rich and powerful young women after her mother's death. Because of the prosperous business deals Her mother had made with different countries in help sustain indigenous populations of people These leaders of those countries highly respected Rose mother. Rose in her carrying out her mother last will and testament, got the opportunity to meet, and be held in high regards as the daughter of such a woman of high moral character and deeds. Rose just wished her father had loved the big heart that her mother truly had, and was not so self-absorbed, they could have made a wonderful and powerful medical team. Rose gathered her bags from the overhead compartment, smiling she began thinking about her next project. Her mother little black book tucked securely in her backpack seemed to have taken on a life of its own. Not wanting to disappoint her father, whom had been waiting for six years for her to return, and take over his private upper Manhattan medical practice. The idea of four walls and ceilings, confinement with the upper crust of society was very scary for Rose to even consider entertaining. It did not matter to Rose that she was one of the wealthiest young women on planet earth. After looking at trees and skies every day, and even most nights, this idea of her father was just overwhelming. Exiting the confinement of the plane brought immediate relief to her. Rose deep in thought was surprised to hear the voice of her father calling to her. "Rose darling!!!" Turning towards the direction of the voice, she sees her father standing with his arms outstretched. "Papa!!!" Rose dropping her shoulder bag, runs into her father's arms crying out his name. At that moment she sees the man that is accompanying her father, looking at her with light grey eyes of interests and delight. Rose peeps from beneath her father's sleeve at him, as her eyes widened in recognition and disbelief..."Michael!!!" Then she remembered today was June 16, and like her mother said distance does makes the heart grows fonder. As she sat on the rocks overlooking the ocean. Rose let her mind wonder back over the past year. The noise of the waves splashing against the rocks, becoming a distance distraction, as her thought of the times she spent with Michael took over. 'Will you wait for me Rose to get my head together? I've made so many mistakes in my life, and meeting you is not one of them." Rose looks up at Michael with tears resting heavy behind her eye lids. Wanting to let them fall, but somehow, she kept her face from letting Michael see the war of emotions going on inside of her. Michael you know that i have grown to care deeply for you these past weeks that we have spent together. I met you at a time when I was on the verge of giving up on love. When I met you i was at a very low place in my life. Hurting and only wanting the pain to stop. Especially dealing with my past love relationship. You came into my life like a whirlwind and wouldn't give up. No matter how hard I tried to keep you at a distance, your persistence finally won me over. Michael I still have trust issues to deal with in my head and heart concerning love, so I also need space and time to continue to heal and find me. Can you be patient enough with me for that? Michael look down into Rose's dark cloudy eyes, kissing her eyelids, he mumbles a deep yes as he pulls her close. "I'll wait Rose, I have to go sort out my sordid past before I can move on, yes we both need time to heal. Rose we'll wait for each other. Let's make a promise to give each other a year from today, June 16th this time next year, and meet up here at this very spot no matter what, ok?" Now a year later, June 16th, Rose sitting on the very rocks, overlooking the ocean along, waiting anxiously for Michael. Wondering if the time they spent apart without communicating had caused him to forget the promise he had made to her. IF that time had caused him to forget her altogether. Would the feeling be the same when they meet? Had someone else came into his life this past year? Did he want and desire her as before? Had Michael truly just moved on with his life? Rose had so many questions running around in her head, that was driving her crazy. Rose mother had told her just this morning, while they were having their girls time together. Rose mother had become total care and home bound because of cancer, told her that sometimes distance makes the heart grow fonder. Even though that never happened between Rose's parents, who lived total separate lives in the same city, even working together for over twenty-two years. Rose Pastor gave her spiritual guidance, equipping and strengthening her as her mother condition got worse. Rose father spent no time or offered any help with her mother. Sitting thinking about her return trip to New York, Rose didn't see the man standing afar off watching her. Then turning and walking away. Knowing in his heart that neither one of them were ready yet…

To be continued in my next Novella Series…Mercy Speaks…2020

www.ingramcontent.com/pod-product-compliance
Ingram Content Group UK Ltd.
Pitfield, Milton Keynes, MK11 3LW, UK
UKHW022220230426
12048UKWH00016BA/955